DISNEY
Winnie the Pooh

It's Fun to Learn

An Arts & Crafts Day

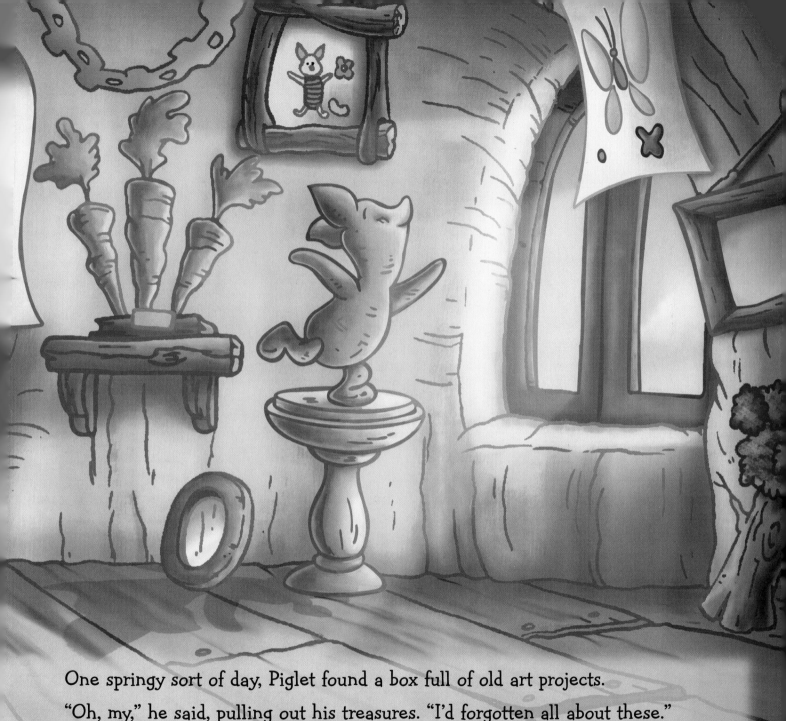

One springy sort of day, Piglet found a box full of old art projects.

"Oh, my," he said, pulling out his treasures. "I'd forgotten all about these."

Piglet had a grand time putting clay sculptures, collages, and homemade frames all over the house.

In fact, Piglet was so pleased with what he'd found that he decided to have his friends over for a little art show.

"Everyone can bring something creative and share!" he said happily.

"Now, about the invitation…hmm…what should it say?"

Piglet went to ask Christopher Robin to write his invitation. Then he began cutting out letters and pasting them down. When he had finished, his invitation read:

Come to Piglet's; save the date!

You won't have very long to wait.

For the show, please do your part...

Make and bring a work of art.

Then off Piglet went to deliver his invitations. His first stop was Pooh's house. Piglet knock-knock-knocked on the door and waited patiently.

Piglet handed Pooh an invitation and told him about his arts and crafts day.

"Everyone will be bringing their very own work of art! It's going to be so much fun!"

"Oh, dear," Pooh replied. "Whatever shall I make?"

Suddenly, Pooh's rumbly tummy gave him an idea.

"I know," said Pooh happily. "I'll paint a picture of a beehive."

Then Pooh had an even better idea. "Why, I'll use honey to paint it," he decided. That way, he could fill his rumbly tummy and paint at the same time.

But the honey was so sticky that Pooh's hands stuck to the paper. And when he tried to pry them loose, his arms, nose, and head got stuck, too.

"Oh, bother," sighed Pooh. "This isn't what I'd planned at all."

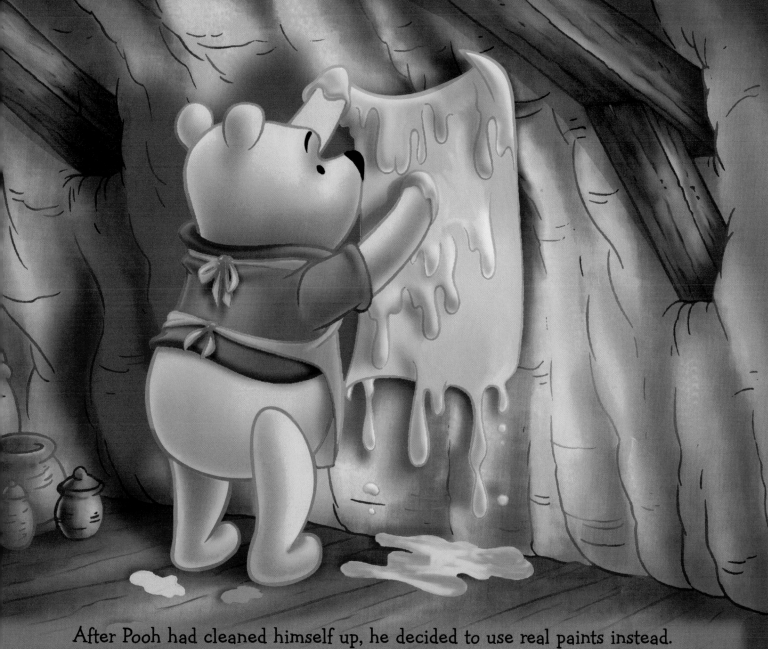

After Pooh had cleaned himself up, he decided to use real paints instead.

But he used so much water that when he hung his painting up to dry, all the colors ran together.

"Think, think, think," said Pooh. "I think, perhaps, I need to think of something else."

So off Pooh went to his thoughtful spot.

While Pooh was busy thinking, Tigger and Eeyore came by.

"Hoo-hoo-hoo!" called Tigger, bouncing along collecting pebbles, flowers, and leaves. "You'll never know me in the marvelicious mask I'm makin' for Piglet's art show. Look!"

Then Eeyore spoke up. "I'm not making anything special—just a stick house made of little twigs."

"You mean you're not painting or drawing a picture?" Pooh asked curiously.

"Don't be ridickerous!" said Tigger, laughing. "A work of art can be anythin' you put a little bounce and imagic-nation into."

"Hmm," said Pooh thoughtfully. "I should put some imagin-er-art into what I like best—honey!"

So Pooh walked along with Tigger and Eeyore thinking about honey. And as he walked, he gathered pebbles, leaves, berries, and twigs…just in case.

But before going home, Pooh dropped in to see what Roo and Kanga were makin[g]
"I'm making a veggible buddy," said Roo, "with radishes for eyes, a carrot for a
nose, and a green bean for a mouth. See? I can make him wear a smile if he's happy o[r]
a frown if he's sad."

"What's Kanga making?" asked Pooh.

"Come outside and see," said Roo.

"It's called a flower chain," Kanga said, showing Pooh how to tie the flowers together. "Mother Nature knew exactly what she was doing when she made every flower a work of art!"

A little while later, Pooh arrived at Rabbit's house.

"Not much time to finish," Rabbit said. "Got to keep working on my bean mosaic. I'm using all sorts of beans—white beans, lima beans, wax beans, string beans, and jelly beans."

"Hmm, I think you've given me an idea, Rabbit," Pooh said. "Thank you."

When Pooh got home, he began to search. "I don't have a garden full of beans," he said. "But I'm sure I can find something in these cupboards that will turn my honey pot into a work of art!"

On the day of Piglet's Art Show, the friends began to gather at Piglet's house.
"How do you like my mask?" asked Tigger. "Don't ya think it makes me
look mystiggerous?"

"What about my beautiful bean mosaic?" said Rabbit.

"Hmm," said Roo. "Maybe I can borrow some of your jelly beans when I want to change the eyes on my veggible buddy."

"That's 'vegetable' Roo, dear," said Kanga.

"Eeyore, this might look good on you." Kanga held up her colorful flower chain.

"Not sure about that," Eeyore said with a sigh.

Soon Pooh showed up at Piglet's house with a honey pot full of flowers.
"This is for you, Piglet, from all of us," Pooh explained happily. "We wanted to thank you for bringing out the 'honey' of an artist in us all!"

And indeed, Piglet had brought out the creativity in every one of his friends. It was the loveliest art show ever in the Hundred-Acre Wood.

Fun to Learn Activity

Oh, my! Tigger, Eeyore, Kanga, Roo, and Rabbit all made such wonderful things to bring to my arts and crafts day. Can you go back through the story and describe what their works of art were made of?

Try making an art project from fun stuff around your house.

RED   GREEN   RED   GREEN   RED   GREEN   RED